S0-BHY-510

Hello Kitty®

Hello Shapes!

illustrated by Higashi Glaser

HARRY N. ABRAMS, INC., PUBLISHERS

One rainy day, Hello Kitty is playing with her toys—a ball that's round and roly, a block that's square for building, a pointy top for spinning! Soon she finds herself daydreaming, and all sorts of shapes start to swirl around in her head . . .

hello circle!

Hello Kitty loves circles, especially when they are fancy balls and circus hoops!

hello square!

Hello Kitty loves squares, especially when she paints pretty pictures on them!

hello triangle!

Hello Kitty loves triangles, especially when they are yummy slices of pizza to share with friends!

hello oval!

Hello Kitty loves ovals, especially the sparkly ones that her ice skates make!

hello rectangle!

Hello Kitty loves rectangles, especially when they are mirrors!

hello diamond!

Hello Kitty loves diamonds, especially when she hits a home run! Go, Hello Kitty, go!

hello star!

Hello Kitty loves stars, especially when they twinkle! Let's make a wish!

hello heart!

Hello Kitty loves hearts, especially the big valentine that she made just for you!

hello crescent!

Hello Kitty loves crescents, especially the moon up above in the twinkling night sky!

1st place
GO TEAM!
home sweet home
Dear Diary
hello shapes!

Hello Kitty loves all the shapes around her! Can you name all the shapes in her room? How many circles, squares, triangles, ovals, rectangles, diamonds, stars, and hearts do you see?

Hello Shapes! Hello Fun!

You can make lots of fun things with shapes! Here are a few ideas to get you started.

Greeting Cards

Fold a piece of paper in half. Use Hello Kitty's stencils to draw shapes with colored pencils, crayons, or markers. Mix shapes to make lots of fun pictures!

Ornaments and Gift Tags

On a piece of heavy paper, trace a shape. Color it in or draw a picture on it if you like. With an adult's help, carefully cut it out with scissors. (For extra fun, use pinking shears!) Tape the decorated shape to a present as a pretty gift tag, or punch a hole near the top and tie a string through it to decorate your room.

Party Streamers

Accordion-fold a piece of colored paper, a little smaller than the width of the stencil shape. Center the stencil between the folded edges. Draw the shape. Cut out the shape, but be careful not to cut the folds off. Unfold your pretty chain of shapes. Tape several end-to-end to make festive party streamers!

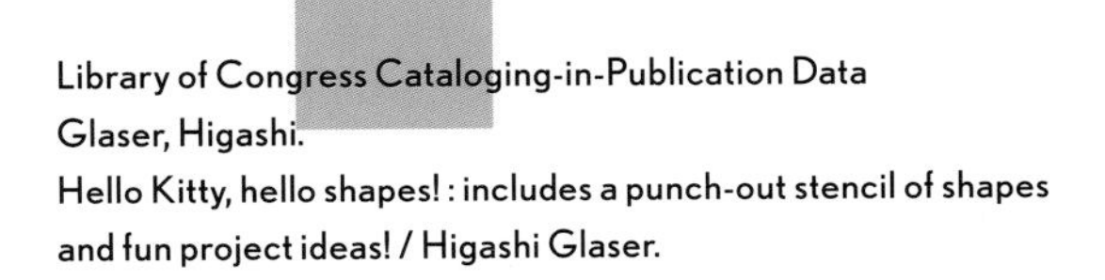
Library of Congress Cataloging-in-Publication Data
Glaser, Higashi.
Hello Kitty, hello shapes! : includes a punch-out stencil of shapes
and fun project ideas! / Higashi Glaser.
p. cm.
Summary: Hello Kitty loves the many different shapes that she encounters
in her everyday life. Includes ideas for shape-related projects.
ISBN 0-8109-4229-1
[1. Shape—Fiction. 2. Cats—Fiction.] I. Title.

PZ7.G48046 Hd 2003
[E]—dc21
2002014069

Hello Kitty® characters, names, and all related indicia are trademarks of Sanrio Co., Ltd.
Used under license. Copyright © 1976, 2003 Sanrio Co., Ltd.

Text and original art copyright © 2003 Harry N. Abrams, Inc.

Published in 2003 by Harry N. Abrams, Incorporated, New York

All rights reserved. No part of the contents of this book may be reproduced
without the written permission of the publisher.

Printed and bound in China
10 9 8 7 6 5 4 3 2 1

Harry N. Abrams, Inc.
100 Fifth Avenue
New York, NY 10011
www.abramsbooks.com

Abrams is a subsidiary of
LA MARTINIÈRE
GROUPE

Hello Kitty's Hello Shapes Stencils

Carefully punch out each shape along the perforated lines. Remove stencil pages from book.
Trace inside the stencil holes to draw different shapes.

Use the punched-out shapes as ornaments or gift tags!